T0166479

WHEREVER YOU LAY YOUR HEAD • *Jane Miller*

Wherever You Lay Your Head

POEMS BY *Jane Miller*

COPPER CANYON PRESS

Printed in the United States of America.

The publication of this book was supported by grants from the Lannan Foundation, the National Endowment for the Arts, and the Washington State Arts Commission. Additional support was received from Elliott Bay Book Company, Cynthia Hartwig, and the many members who joined the Friends of Copper Canyon Press campaign. Copper Canyon Press is in residence with Centrum at Fort Worden State Park.

LIBRARY OF CONGRESS CATALOGING-IN-PUBLICATION DATA

Miller, Jane, 1949–
Wherever you lay your head / by Jane Miller.
  p. cm.
ISBN 1-55659-128-4 (alk. paper)
1. Title.
PS3563.I4116 W48 1999
811'.54 – DC21   99-6032
                              CIP

9 8 7 6 5 4 3 2 FIRST PRINTING

COPPER CANYON PRESS
Post Office Box 271
Port Townsend, Washington 98368
www.ccpress.org

ACKNOWLEDGMENTS

Grateful acknowledgment is made to the editors of the following journals in which these poems first appeared:

The American Poetry Review, CutBank, Fence, Green Mountains Review, Luna, New American Writing, The Ohio Review, The Seattle Review, and *Sonora Review.*

Lines quoted from Henry Wadsworth Longfellow, "The Song of Hiawatha," *Longfellow's Complete Poetical Works,* Houghton Mifflin Co., Cambridge Edition, 1893; John Donne, "Holy Sonnets (xiv)," *The Complete Poetry and Selected Prose of John Donne,* edited by Charles M. Coffin, The Modern Library, Random House, New York, 1952.

Cover art is *Yui* (Station 17) of *"The Fifty-three Stations of the Tōkaidō," Prints by Hiroshige in the James A. Michener Collection,* Honolulu Academy of the Arts, 1991. (There were many sets of prints. The Michener Collection alone owns ten sets, including this *gojūsan-tsugi,* Fifty-three Stations, a half *ōban* set of vertical prints published by Muraichi between 1849 and 1852, popularly known as "Jinbutsu Tōkaidō" since figures are stressed over landscape.) The commentary of Muneshige Narazaki provides wonderful aid along the route in *Hiroshige, The Fifty-three Stations of the Tōkaidō in the Masterworks of Ukiyo-e* ["pictures of the floating world"], English adaptation by Gordon Sager (Kodansha International Limited, Tokyo and New York, 1969).

Also see Note on the Cover, page 81.

Contents

FOR *Jacqi Tully*

The Flying Fish and Lily of May

In an hour as yet unspent,
whose very name "forget-me-not"
suggests a golden age of ordinary
people out to see the cherry
flowers gather in the brightness of the flames,

the day
grows dark reminding every guest
a guild of poets – who are dressed
in February as plum blossoms
and in August as the tremulous

camellia – accompanies romance
and makes of circumstance a rendezvous; in such hour
as deltaic rivers slice the city written
with fine beams of light, and steamy images
rise under bridges down straits

to the sea, I shall be dreaming all the while awake
to hear asked, "How did we bear the pain?" and the world
answer, "Everyone was in it, too,"
such that it will have been miraculous
to have lived our love and sing of it to you.

Probability of an Event

The best place to be is in one
of the restaurants north of the bridge
on the west side along the river,
or on a chartered pleasure boat.
Skiffs with single lanterns
wander among the cruisers
selling food and drink. Under the chill
moonlit sky, one can rent a ride
and be carried, or walk wearing a hood
with the sensation felt as a child
moving through the great open windy world
of mutilated statues and spoiled food
and never understanding.
The traveler from village to village
and from village to town in the rain
eventually is found illumined
by streetlamps in a nightless city,
in a mud puddle's yellow bands.
More than a hundred houses
along the embankment,
each with a woman peeping from behind
a screen, laying out her combs
and fixing her French knot

with a mahogany hairpin.
It is legend that creates place.
The burning of swamp gas
and glow of luminescent fungi.
Otherwise she carries a straw mat
to an alley and she covers her disease
with foundation and rouge.
Tissue paper for the act.
The yearning of the traveler
is fire for the world's
largest wooden city.

2

The firewatcher is eliminated
in a world of supernatural powers.
The core of light builds slowly.
Stalls of bear, monkey, boar, and deer,
and otter and fox and wolf and weasel
appear along the quay,
the chemistry of five AM.
Roof boats and uncovered taxis vanish.
The mountain lion is down from the mountain
on a hook. In a hurry,
two pairs of sandals forgotten.
The green blinds are raised.

Day is a model of the world
so different from the phantom
seen before,
and that perhaps one may hope
never to see again,
and can explain what looks like water
on the road is sky.
The hot air is next to the road's
surface, say, by five in the afternoon,
citizens scurrying home
with mattresses on their heads
and sashes around their waists

trailing children,
and the matter simply becomes
more and more violently atomized.
A tiny pedestal of a steel tower remains
on which the test bomb had been mounted.
The blast has vaporized the tower
and fused the surface of the surrounding
sands into jade-green glass.
The figures of the day in a phenomenal chain
reaction. The legend is in the light.

Background Paper

The time is four o'clock in the morning
when the wooden gates of the city open.
Spindly-legged porters bear two heavyweight wrestlers
crossing the river early to avoid their public.
By the time they reach the mountaintop,
snow will pile up on their paper umbrellas.
This panorama is seen now most often
on matchboxes in the world's most crowded city.
The sagging chests of the wrestlers,
the torn silks of the river,
the gateposts and the snow of the original woodcut
toss like dolls through the air
along a scenic route. One could take a month or a year,
living by spending or stealing. If you were
robbed and honest, you lived very badly
on your way home. If you were homeless,
you lived very badly and traded your body
for the favorite food of your favored client,
starving on plum cakes. In the worst cases,
it could take a very long time to die young and nameless.

2

When "Mike" exploded in the South Pacific
it took fifteen minutes for the shock to travel
under the Pacific Basin to the California coast
into a basement room where a seismograph was writing
with a beam of light on photographic film
its story of peaks and valleys and the pounding
of ocean waves onto shore. It took some time
but eventually Albert Einstein said,
"We must bring the facts about nuclear energy
to the village square," meaning
someone was finally going to explain why
after the test the captain's shoes were "too hot"
to let him off the ship. If an earthquake
disturbs the surplus now housed, or if, say,
some saggy-chested trucker making a living hauling
plutonium gets sleepy and dishonors his charge,
then the innocent
need only face the psychic
fireball that sears their lifeless bodies,
whereas we shall toss through the air like dolls.

New Year's Stations

The ghostly pilgrim
of heaven between walled crags
and the new lime moon –
general tone of gray which
white snow generously spots

Teahouse maids in green,
purple, vermilion, yellow –
an ornamental
temple gate in red ocher
one's eyes pulled into the smoke

Travel notes jotted
between cups of cool sake
and steaming miso –
approaching fifty lanterns
one should recognize one's fate

STATION 4

> Red apricot trees –
> light from the fire pokes out
> green of the cedar
> here the paper lantern throws
> a patch of blue on one's coat

STATION 5

> Stopping for a smoke
> under wobbling eagles' nests
> a peasant woman
> borne on the froth of a wave
> sits among pine trees on straw

STATION 6

> Small clam boats at right
> sailboat with a canvas screen
> of a family's crest
> each headed toward the checkpoint
> foreground – two blind street singers

STATION 7

Roadside teahouse famed
for sweet rice cakes in oak leaves –
a second boat stops
two wrestlers being carried
New Year's Eve across water

STATION 8

A family of three
weary pilgrims hurrying
to their night's lodging –
a number of fires around
means a good harvest this year

STATION 9

Wearing summer robes
seated before the full moon
beauties drink from boat-
shaped porcelain bowls – fishing
boats hide seaweed gatherers

STATION 10

> In front of the shrine
> a large nettle tree to which
> foxes arrive late
> New Year's Night – change into their
> formal attire and pray

STATION 11

> Because of the strange
> figurations of branches
> one may look into
> a pond and city beyond –
> an old man's staff in each hand

STATION 12

> Light from a fire
> smoke from the farther bonfire
> and light from the lamp
> tied to the rider's saddle
> shape the running courier

STATION 13

Jig-jag path crossing
a town flanked by a slow hill –
a passing shower
tiger rain falls on four blind
men following each other

STATION 14

A solitary
boatman poling his timber
seen along the banks
through falling snow which piles
up on his hat and straw coat

STATION 15

Kids roughing their dogs
man leading a tired horse
farmer carrying
loads on a pole in a dream –
water flooded with moonlight

STATION 16

    Those in silhouette
    protect themselves with rush mats
    from the storm – cedars
    cover the shrine the faint cone
    of the mountain quivers white

STATION 17

    Not quite three years old
    he is already sleeping
    on his mother's back
    custom covers the new twins
    in purple shawls – foxfire!

STATION 18

    Fireworks at night
    a flowering flash of mist
    one's fondness for food
    and drink causes one to slip
    into the icy streambed

STATION 19

A flock of snow geese
entertaining beauties pauses
and spirits off – glimpse
their pretty red underwear
as they cross the monkey bridge

Firewatcher

If every experience is shaped by a fantasy
how does matter behave when we pound
sufficient fissionable material

to obtain a chain reaction
normal men weakened
advocate digging a hole

two or three feet deep
crawl in cover one another somehow
and wait

for red from saffron
blue from indigo black from charcoal
white from clay and from clamshells

whosoever shall recognize
the deepest sources of the Bomb's grasp on us
shall retrieve them

shall bury the burn victims
and with the unconscious birds discover the bread
and enjoy the yam paste for which the town is famous

we are a district of sticks and swords
of earthquakes and views
the son of the fire warden accedes at age ten

he has time between fires to study the old masters
to see the world foregrounded and the future achieved
though the traveler search in vain

for the blue boatman poling his raft
for the smoke from the brazier
the feeling of liveliness is familiar

not for use in war
where armies are locked in battle
but dropped on populated zones

the day before the bombing is a Sunday
many who have gone outside haven't returned
not a few seek nightly refuge outside the limits

special units are inside
construction workers and forced laborers
in the Heavy Industries fierce fire

whipped winds drive the wounded winds
irradiated rain rips from the cloud
down mown fields schools town halls and temples

whosoever has not seen the conflagration
must study the old masters
distracted from care by the beauty of nature

in the distance the boy leads a horse up a mountain
he has lost his mother and father
to natural painful causes

runners in relays expressing messages
ask of the city
why fish hang at the entrance to the only inn

Site Y

The fireball gathers speed like a tumbleweed
ignites breakfast coals dying out on braziers
sweeps fire lanes

care begins with those alone
who don't know their own names
next the orphaned elderly

the quantum theory is troubled
if you calculate roughly
it gives a reasonable answer

if you compute accurately
the correction you thought small
is in fact large is in fact infinity

hardtack rations
two balls of cooked rice per person
all easily explained

gravity and radioactivity mysterious
white cell counts drop
the cuckoo flies by night

above a river shaded by willows
a captain of industry and a distinguished scientist
happy and panicked

trek through a snowstorm in May
and come upon a site for a laboratory
a desert flooded in forget-me-nots

the rest is history
a large boat with curtains
banners and fur-tipped lances

carries a major personage
quoted as saying
a country like ours

in any real sense cannot survive
if we are afraid of our people
careless with money fond of drinking

contemptuous of authority
an old painter sets out on his last trip
chooses a perch among the brightest maples

The Grand Waterfall Plunges
Unbending into the Pool Below

with only a tiny wreath of waves.
It is 1942 and Edward Teller pushes back from his station,
uncomfortable since his lamb lunch
in the cafeteria, and unbuckles a notch.
His stomach gases are on fire.
What fat he hasn't wiped from his hands
has greased and blurred his slide rule.
He hasn't stopped into the washroom
because he is preoccupied calculating
that a nitrogen reaction
could kindle an explosion beyond
the team's control.
For this bomb
Oppenheimer and Compton
stake the odds at three times
in a million. Here are men who feel
they distinguish among sleep,
delusion, and reality,
tiny flashes of mica
on a bare-branched green pine.
Foxes leap under the branches
spitting flames,
and from their height and merriment
farmers foretell harvest.
Countdown begins in darkness.
Dawn quiet over the Oscura hills to the east.

General Farrell prays the test
is a boy – a winner – rather than a girl.
A small sun slowly rises
surrounded by blue light
fixed to earth by a charcoal stem.
Silence. Then the blast. In God's eyes,
tiny flashes of mica leap spitting flames.
"First of all,"
Teller, the heavy, confides, "I have no hope
of clearing my conscience." The fungal blue glow
sits and thinks of Winston Churchill
in an unzipped siren suit, hearing the success
of the experiment, sucking a cigar and smiling
through a facsimile of atomic smoke.
People march from twin cities in a dream
we are at once forbidden to see
and at the same time required.
A charred common skin
at least someone and probably many
could have saved,
figures climbing through a craggy garden
toward a bright pavilion,
small factories, and shops.
Two men indulge in a comic dance with fans.
Ladies chat, drawing in their parasols
to absorb the warm summer sun.

Rising Smoke

One obeys nature and thinks of the rest of the journey
in straw sandals and paper hat. The leaves larger
and the light longer. I could do it in my sleep,
my head a roadway peppered with mountain passes.

My brother disappears with his lights on,
my mother, at eighty, travels between
the heavy rains of the four seasons.
What I imagine happens sets not one inn in place,

nor puts our dead father to rest. The air is chilly,
despite a feast and a fire. I'm the one to say it
about myself, I feel like a servant wading across,
relieved of possessions.

It doesn't hurt to write, it's as difficult as learning
to read a glance. The head of a fawn? Shark teeth?
A dream is snatched from me, then emptiness,
its carved door broken into.

An afternoon of one glimpse of a narrow bay.
A guardhouse stands at the end
of a bridge. Sweep of lute strings.
This is the spot grown children abandoned

their aging mothers,
a young man kissed his love good-bye on the forehead,
a young woman returned without composing a single line
an old woman not in her own bed.

In Such a Way That Nothing
Could Go Wrong

A low stratum of mushroom cloud
begins shortly to move over the park
in a north-northwesterly direction
& twenty or thirty minutes later
to rain radioactive
building block & human remains
onto still living stick figures
& thus with a fireball to evaporate
a paradise of hackberry trees

Two waitresses pedaling to a noodle shop downtown
see the last of the freshness of dawn
fume into the regular traffic & trade of oblivion
a hundred thousand fall in the city like blossoms along a riverbank
some crawl burned
& faceless into the rising river
poor memory
too tired to rest
especially in summer or in the sun

School

A Hispanic gentleman familiar
with piñon in the adobe fireplace
shovels on soft coal
which pours acrid smoke
through the ventilators in the mirror-image
apartments of the evacuated
Los Alamos, New Mexico, Ranch School,
straightening slowly. *Bueno.*
Kitty Oppenheimer's name is on a list
of wives waiting for her maid to arrive
by bus from the valley this weekday morning,
and is awake enough in her log and stone house
on a quiet road partly shielded
by shrubs and a small garden
to smell the regular disturbance again.

She and her husband haven't the time
to advise the janitor of his error,
or to enjoy the pine-covered promontory,
or the Rio Grande Valley, or hike the old trails
of the Valle Grande,
or even to gaze out beyond the fence and the military patrol
toward the Pajarito Plateau,
because they live in a magic place which vanishes
in the blowing dust of construction this summer,

and they can only retrieve it
by getting beyond the sun behind the Jemez skyline
along bad roads ten miles back
by hairpin turns and precipitous drops,
and that is impossible now. It is dawn
and a long day ahead, the nearest railroad
sixty miles away, and the many secluded
canyons and mesas host experiments
beyond the broad two-mile-long mesa
which spits up the bus this morning.
Buenos días.

Here is pregnant Anna,
firm and big as a gourd.
Anna is using the money
for her family, who cannot believe
the price gringos will pay
so she can ride the bus into the country
a few hours a day to polish the laboratories,
resident quarters, and dining hall.
Anna has heard that Kitty's husband is lost
in a mountain snowdrift or in the desert.
She knows because everyone knows
he is searching for a secret
site three hundred miles south

in the desolate Jornada del Muerto, near Alamogordo,
where anyone goes who wants to
die for a day. *Dios mío.*

Anna loves Kitty because she is fair
and Kitty loves Anna because she is dear.
They come from far away and meet
between the familiar and the unknown,
to which Kitty's husband gives the name
Trinity, from "Batter my heart, three-person'd God,"
a line little understood
and which might otherwise do some good,
muchas gracias.
We fly straight in at medium height
at rather low speed over the city
and drop one bomb with the energy
of fifteen thousand tons of TNT,
killing more than a hundred thousand people
and wounding at least a hundred thousand people.
We destroy the medium-sized city.
It is not a question of one bomb.
It is a question of ten, and then
one hundred, and then a thousand,
and then, maybe, one hundred thousand.
We know or, rather, do not know,

but think that it is not a question
of ten thousand tons
but of one hundred thousand
and then a million tons, or ten million,
and then, perhaps, of one hundred million.
When Grant, at Appomattox, looked beyond
the slaughter to nature and to time
he could tell Lee to let his troops keep
their horses because they would need them
for plowing in the early spring.
Oppenheimer himself drops by briefly

during the celebration at the school
on August 15, 1945, after hostilities cease
of a sudden, as planned, after we drop
a plutonium bomb on Nagasaki
and a uranium bomb on Hiroshima,
only to find a level-headed young scientist
vomiting in the shrubs,
to whom he says, and who can in no way
emerge to consciousness to hear him
nor be able to entertain the instant of brilliance
required to recommend him to us
and to this place, much like the future,
in which the poor body is defeated

and the spirit transformed,
where all has been reclassified
and all are being
informed of our acts,
"The reaction has begun."
Jesus Cristo.

"Dave's Dream" (B-29 Bomber)

From where he stands
over the ubiquitous flames
three hundred and some odd
miles away, layering mesquite
among his toxic coals
for the perfect finish,

it looks like somebody's opened
a refrigerator at night
in daylight, and this purplish
pink glow like the light from home
appliances throughout the remote
Southwest and beyond, Vegas,

the City of Angels, etc.,
this hot light, from which he's divided
by a cyclone fence, is another
successful experiment to etch
the retinas of rabbits and desert rats,
many of which lurch blindly

now toward his barbecue,
his miniature smoking earth, curl up
on his radioactive chaise

and beg for the remaining
pierced, marinated, charred,
spit-flamed and rotated

on this earth to be saved.

"Fat Man" and "Little Boy"

We rent the apartment
in the Land of Enchantment
of one David Greenglass, deceased,
209 High Street, righting the globe,
the ashtrays and dishes, bomb
sketches, and thirty-one packages
of cherry Jell-O,

halved to match the other spy's half
and reunited now in the demimonde
of children's innocent round
red cherry bombs with little green
fuse stems,

which brighten the setting at the birth
of the white man's plan
on a Formica table in the kitchen
of a one-bedroom in a small town
at ground zero. We have arrived

at a place in a chain
of ridges at Three Rivers
where the Anasazi live
in drawings of cougars, birds, lions, and fish,
cougars, birds, lions, and fish

they killed with hook and spear,
and ate, and worshiped,
a place inside the furnace

of the Rio Grande and Sierra Oscura,
and we have a nanosecond
to dismantle every bolt and rivet
of "Little Boy" and "Fat Man,"
Greenglass's arsenal
of aeronautical symbols
alive on this table
as if he'd breathed life
into tin soldiers
or cowboys and Indians,
except he wishes he were more dead
because of how many more dead
he succeeded in freeing from one life
and recommending to another, superannuating
God, whose guests now wake
Greenglass between every blink
with an explosion.

Hurry up.
Although he wishes he were more dead,
rather than simply buried

in the history of weaponry
and espionage and revenge,
he knows our secret
sin of commission now that we've turned
the key and entered the temple.
Rather than drop the bomb,
lift the shade and swiftly turn off the light,
we can barely imagine our selves
without a victim,
a complexity in fake lamé
who has one finger
on the release. Welcome to the demimonde

where we get to sing
about anything
because we worshiped
our recreation,
on a sentimental mission to return
our souls to our bodies.
We are back at the sketchpad
scared to death,
scorched by the metaphor
of a "Fat Man" and a "Little Boy"
high on fossil fuel
in a designer jet timed to regurgitate

an ancient admixture,
and we can barely distinguish ourselves

by denying its poetry
and denying it life.

Blast Site

An airman, trying not to fall
through turbulence coming into Kirtland
from 17,000 feet with a 42,000-pound
Mark 17 load, does grab, by mistake,
the sphincter that releases
his B-36 bomb-bay door face.
Mr. Lieutenant Midnight Memory,
flying the sky in his small craft
nearby, May 22, 1937,
remembers there isn't a thimble of wind

the Friday anyone drops
a dud in the dirt
outside Albuquerque,
many times the distance, in miles,
the amount of plutonium, the number of tons
and a potential number of times
more powerful than the blast
at Hiroshima. We are pilots
of a small plane in flight
poised with Mr. Memory

over Albuquerque, reciting in a trance
the fact of the bomb's being,
by chance, not fully armed, when

like delicate human
stomach-lining blown sky high,
coyote liquefy
as an invisible blizzard
of one hundred percent Agave
El Jimador Tequila Reposado bottles
bursts in thin air. Forevermore

concatenated with Central Command,
sagebrush and tumbleweed de-happen
when the plane hits one
flier's fucking hyperventilation.
We rip, on purpose,
through this bomb-bay door
and we come face to face
with the creation,
perfectly restored,
of a twenty-five-foot-wide

twelve-foot-deep forbidden city.

Seed Bed

Prickly pears guard the site.
Dressed in fatigues,
we return to a desert
covered in snow.
Years of fires
have refashioned the Sandias
but, closer in, Albuquerque Airport
blinks day and night
such that no one could mistake it.
It's windy.
Suspended from nylon filament,
our plane won't hold still.
One intern drafts black smoke,
others tamp the ash.
The ground is naked where it was peeled
from its vegetation back then,
creating the depression.
The nature of the original
cover-up requires events
be reinvented, down to the decal
on the jet and the hummingbird nests.
Now our childhood fantasy
B-36 is free to land
in a bed of handmade snow
and to blow the aloe and lavender,
hung like Christmas tinsel
with spiders and lizards,

several hundred thousand
millimeters from the restored
rats, squirrels, moles, raw ores,
and, finally, the molten core
of riven polyurethane.
Nothing happens, and for no particular reason
it doesn't hurt anyone
when a manufactured wind scatters
props and Styrofoam cups.
When we miss the runway,
we can only tear a gash
per square inch times the power
of the explosive which, in our case,
is the sizzling instant
everyone realizes we have grown up
completely overnight
and things have become personal
as well as professional.
Therefore I lay me down with you
to contemplate the warm snow
and the red gel on the windows.
Suffering is still cordoned off.
Our creation is a flash
coming off the fluorescent
of our gibbous motel, a mille-feuille
of research papers falling like snow.

Green Valley

I can fly here in my car
the morning my brother sells
capped Texas oil wells
to the elderly, and can dine
in one of two Valley motel establishments
and hear him call our waitress's name
because he has noticed her laminated
tag affixed to her foreshortened blouse
this air-conditioned Thursday,
following the game plan as habitually as the enchanted
elders executed eighteen holes earlier
and every yesterday of their retirement from this
deteriorating situation, lunch,
wherein I have placed my canned soup
and my bottled water order
and am drifting patiently like a plane
going down, nothing wrong, no warning,
just an intuition about my adult years veering
from the light into the glare
and the accompanying mountain wall there,
which contains Green Valley as unremarkably and inevitably
as I have this stranger in my life,
investing in the absolute without knowing
I am going to be let down
and made to live what I was thinking

as the mountain approached, or feeling,
before being saved from the everlasting
heat of one hundred and ten degrees
for the daily heat of one hundred and nine in Tucson
with the lightning and thunder of the oblivion
of our father gone and our mother mistaken,
driving the earth around Miami
in the slow lane of creation
with her pupils dilated,
circling her condominium, a cataract
being pulled across her eyes like matting
protecting a manicured course from natural
forces and, all the unsuspecting while,
I am shamelessly pulverizing
crackers and squeezing the life out of a lemon
into the lukewarm bloody soup.
Float now
through the blue skies of my brother's
eyes to the music of geologic
time; listen to the voice
from the sealed well.
This is what has driven me
in the opposite and equally depleted
direction early, carefully listening to fusion
and concentrating on every emotion,

rushing from the riches of one
brother's pledge of celestial pleasure
to one brotherless blue silk suit of sunny weather.

Views of Edo

The placement of the clouds is no accident.
From the right side of a Southwest Airlines 737 heading west
you see the beautiful white deposits
perspiring like athletes
against a gray-brown landscape,
and you see the Rio Puerco
perspiring like a sleeping god,
carrying water along Interstate 40
contaminated with ten to a hundred times
the maximum allowable plutonium,

and if you squint you see the corpses
of roadrunners along 285,
the old Stinson cattle trail,
and Jim Stinson, manager, New Mexico Land and Livestock,
perspiring under his felt hatband,
a toy cowboy driving 20,000 cattle
in eight herds from Texas to the Estancia Valley
like insects across the open plains
between pines at a Christmas tree farm.

There's a spring-green lizard
whose infrastructure you see
in the ribs of a dying saguaro,
low desert brush disgorged for a branch of road,

crawling anyway toward your shadow
with its spirit,
frog eyes and dinosaur legs and carcass
toward your shadow as it spreads
across square gray rock.
It stops carrying its weight
mid-crawl, and you see the scales
catch the sun, tail up like a jet,
your eyes on an eye on one side of its nuked head,
and you swim for a second
before you see the moon is dry,
before you see the cataract of a window of hell.
You see yellow coveralls and a gas mask
gesturing from the relative safety of the inside

of a truck smeared with clay,
and 14 fifty-gallon drum
TRUPACT II containers of
more than 15 grams of plutonium,
of which one-millionth
gram is cancerous.
You see
22 million tons of uranium tailings
piled 100 feet high over 245 acres
seeping into the aquifer under the site

of the Homestead Mining Company, Cibola County,
and you see zinc, lead, and copper tailings snake
into the earth. Ten thousand or so men in T-shirts
and space suits are getting off shift at
Lawrence Livermore National Laboratory
in the balding Northern California hills;
the Savannah River Plant, among the weeping willows,
Aiken, South Carolina; the Nevada Test Site;
the Y-12 Plant, Oak Ridge, Tennessee;
Rocky Flats, Golden, Colorado;
the Pantex Plant, Amarillo, Texas;
you see them fan out like ants;
you see everything living and dead
laid out on a map of the United States
crawling with radiation.
You see the trusted

face of a calculator
counting the drums and dumps,
and the unaging face of plutonium,
white as a marble sea, asleep
beside you everywhere you go,
a giant pillow
timed to explode.
"All they've told us is if

there's an emergency we call
the special number and someone will
be here in an hour and a half.
BUT WHAT IF THERE'S A WRECK
AND THE DRIVER IS PINNED IN THE CAB,
or something? Even if I don't know
the site is contaminated, I'm not
going to wait an HOUR AND A HALF."
The ground is ticking
under the eyelid of soil
under the pilings.
You're flying so high
you look still.
You see a summer thunderstorm
because you see miraculously
what is next, moving through space
above central storage.
You see the polished heads of the MX and Trident
through spindly mesquite and furry sage.

You see the present in the sunburnt
features of the passengers,
and when you rest your eyes you close in
on a trawler in a small boat
mostly hidden,

his hand pressing the bottom
to brace him against a rocking
flash of rain.
In a straw-thatched teastall on the left,
the owner is boiling water.
Chilly evening in late fall.
A man stirring a fire.
Two men warming their behinds against it.
A black-robed priest with an umbrella-shaped mat headcovering
walks away slowly, smoking a short-bowled pipe.
The porch of a restaurant behind.
Masts of boats and a flock of geese
obstruct the clouded moon.
Two women with their hair held up by combs
whisper together by the light of a paper-thin lamp.
For a few coins a couple of peasants
are given floor to sleep on
after a day of steady walking
and a few sticks of cherry wood on which to cook.
The pilgrim in white is no doubt on his way
to a shrine because he is carrying
a mask of a deity with a large nose.

Speed Queens

Into the dark dry mouth of the five-hundred-pound behemoth
the veteran Interstate Nuclear Cleaning and Laundering manager drops
his next dull hot load of irradiated clothes,
so perforce the stainless steel centerpiece of an endless round of pick up
& decontamination & delivery
of coveralls, of cloth hoods, of rubber gloves & respirators
grinds its teeth on a residential block in Pleasanton, California,
a small thriving city
in the temperate Livermore Valley,
masticating docilely.
Manager Craig Connelly would like to go on
smoking & thinking,
making money for himself & his family,
Monday through Friday, without worries,
stating at a city hearing,
"I've been in this business for eleven years,
& I don't glow." The many spent flecks
keep barely visible thoughts to themselves,
& he to himself, or there will be the devil to pay,
& therefore the giant machine & the dwarf
each lost in his own smoke
turn over their respective thoughts
& into the heady neighborhood air
blow them mightily.
Manager Connelly is about to return home

in ankle-deep snow without passengers
when he sees them, barefoot,
on raised wooden sandals,
& though they appear to him
to need transport as powerfully as he needs their fare,
they don't accept his offer.

Space Trash

Downtown is deserted.
These teenagers of America are on their backs listening
to tailings spill into the Rio Puerco.
The night sky has a low ceiling.
It is a giant wide
military theater
a honeycombed cell
in which one hears
the celestial bell better
than in high school
or in the kitchen
dishwashing at WENDY's.
The accompanying drums thunder.
Satellites star the city.
These large children are at home
listening to the great father and the loving mother
of the universe on a drug so strong
that when the great mother and loving father
warn the deer of the hunters
and make rain that the rivers cleanse themselves,
they hear the butterflies of their brains
burn out gently like satellites
that have entered their screens
and eventually their dreams.
They are dreaming

By the shining Big-Sea-Water
Downward through the evening twilight
In the days that are forgotten
From the land of sky blue waters

and are happy smoking
despite the chill. They are thinking of all the ways
their ancestors described the heavens
so nothing would move ever
and no one disappear
and all manner of shape and texture
suffice the imagination
when the ceiling lowers again imperceptibly.
The bride of the sky hunches so her headdress fits.
Sagittarius shortens his big toe,
a thimble of megastars fills
the little cup. "What have I done
in my time alone?" someone panics.
His friends bring him home again
to the voice of his mother's heart
closer every instant
like flaming stars
nuclear garbage
and the new year.
Hallelujah!
Love everlasting blows over

the perfumed hills and valleys of the heavens.
It dazzles the unlucky
legends of the sky
who, like angels,
can neither create nor destroy,
while here on earth
young men and women stare idly.
Finally they call it a night,
slouch to their convertible low riders,
and drive to their separate beds
by the shores of Gitche Gumee
by the shining Big-Sea-Water,
where the nightmare begins.

"'Til the End of Time"

Beauty and barrenness all around
when they leave the Quonset hut
after the briefing –

twelve men climb through the hatch
the plane lumbers down the runway
(in the sand and coral nearby
test fuselages burn)

slow on the ground and graceful in air
it burrows through the soft Pacific night
"June Is Bustin' Out All Over" on the radio stateside

under the B-29 the atomic bomb is not a handsome weapon
dull gray gunmetal
nose tungsten steel
the plane weaves through columns of cumulus cloud

breaking to view the dark ocean
the moon and bright tropical stars
some distance from the drop

women wearing dresses and kimonos
burn according to the shading of the patterns
on the pages of an open book some very far distance away
the blank paper seems untouched

but the heat-absorbing letters neatly burn out
some walk with their burned arms up
away from their burned bodies

Gnome Site

A young Paguate wipes the grit
into his eyes before he shoots
and misses

manages his own rebound
his back to the basket
pirouettes

breathlessly right
blind to his defender
leaps and hangs in the air

as if on a balcony gazing out
over green fields of purple wisteria
the ball quivers and drops

there's the lingering question how
on everyone's lips
the giant layered in dust

plies back and forth
like a boatman in mist
in bold garments

which echo the blossoms
of his youth
standing immobile on the water

fixing his pole in the river
and his gaze on the far shore
he casts another impossible glance

and sails the sphere
through air the color of his beloved
cornmeal a golden rainfall

our first visit to the pueblo
we can still see
the eastern and southern apple

and melon orchards
and fields of beans
The Jackpile Uranium

Mine blew out
a perfect accident
dazzling the villagers

leaving a dusting
of treasure
the wind picks up

hangs in the air
twirls and drops
on anyone's shoulders and hair

The Sea Is Light in a
Passing Shower

Sweetness makes us forget
the time we aren't gods.

Clang of iron
skillet and tin dishes.

It starts out dry in winter
and never rains or snows.

We go into town
for flour, sugar, and beans,

and for a book
we find the time

to read images and messages,
which see as we see burning

sands and mountains and Geronimo
bloodied by Buffalo Soldiers,

never knowing what hit,
like fragile corn by drought.

When men and women walk again
the springtime of the world,

climb the canyon, die
by poison and by firepower,

they awaken as someone else living
in Paradise with an empty cup.

From then until now,
the sea is light in a passing shower.

The Voiceless Beagles of Davis

A barge steams from Concord Station
under six bridges, through the Carquinez Strait,

and into San Pablo Bay with another safe delivery
by ancient sailors, who project in golden sunset

the silhouette of youth next to the latest
small bazooka-like device, "Davy Crockett,"

representing America, such that when I step out
on my porch in ancient summer light,

in spring, Wednesday
at the end of the century

in which, with few exceptions,
those who favored a prior warning to the enemy

later argued for more weapons,
while those who recommended the bomb

spoke after war of disarmament,
so all-clear is the dusk it can drown

the silent howling of the beagles
being zapped with 60 millirems

of radiation at the nearby campus,
their cords cut

so they won't bark their sacrifice at bicyclists going by.
Whereas the vacuum of the moon prevents life,

I shall lay a spray of small flowers down
at the end of advanced time

because I want someone to recognize
the bergamot, orange blossom, peach, and rose

in the humble gardens on the streets of Venus
when we are forced to kill again with clubs.

The Sushi Eaters

We are the bourgeoisie
in clean cotton kimonos
with lacquered plates and chopsticks

our deceased father Walt pinches a California roll
our mother Florence nibbles yellowtail
on a torpedo of rice

We wear cool sunglasses to the parade
on the fifth day of the fifth month
boys hoist banners of painted carp

citizens throw back their catch
off crowded bridges into cold streams
lost souls surface in ceremonial robes

Our host dresses in strips of kelp
with an upside-down basket on his head
on the brim of which sits citrus

huge wood pestle stuck in his sash
white puffs of plum blossom
peep from the garden behind the teahouse

The paddies beyond are still stubble
young Dr. Teller's face like
tuna illumined with wasabi and soy

suntanned and oiled with protection
against his test bomb – fire eaters!
One is forced to travel on crutches

Yellow Cake

The faithful park recreational vans
and lay their miniature missiles
off Highway 70 in the red hue
of the sanctuary at White Sands,
and all with graceful youthfulness
raise their arms heavenward.

Our favorite comedians imitate us,
risking a good dusting on the grounds
of the Nike-Hercules Missile Monument.
They record the magical
unthinkable events taking place
by bowing to the stone and reciting
its contaminated poem,
"When Thy Mother Dies in Thine Arms."

The only animal on the place
is a prize Guernsey
dropping a patty, foreground,
like the great draftsman Hiroshige's
large horse standing in dung
in *One Hundred Famous Views of Edo,*
very dull and neutral like the real color
tea, wood, or straw.

Our favorite comedians stand around
glowing like the sun
and talk to a grim bronze plaque
about the recipe for yellow cake,
uranium for the fuel pads
our Lord faces earthward.
Every quiet afternoon

the grounds are alive.
When thy mother is anointed
and dies in thine arms,
we put to rest the oracle
in the ore of the reactor
by grinding and pressing and entering it
as pellets under honeyed skies'
sulfuric register.

The New Mexico State Fair
black-and-white milker
dropping a patty
with youthful gracefulness
pastures among real people
who live in the clouds.

Summer Solstice Stations

STATION 1

Yellow kites over
the nightless summer city
homeless shouldering
large blue packs of newspapers
for morning delivery

STATION 2

Prisoners awake
on the priceless blue coastline
tumble the western
gatelock as dawn tolls up last
night's eucalyptus profits

STATION 3

Surreal things happen
first waking is illusion
olallieberries
from the Berkeley Bowl to home
then the normal world of dream

STATION 4

> Pages, pike bearers,
> umbrello, and hat bearers
> talk when they're tired
> returning to the real world
> youthful heroic fictions

STATION 5

> Shopping in the mall
> for exercise equipment
> large ships drift ashore
> invention or fantasy
> men with long exploding guns

STATION 6

> Among the figures
> crossing Golden Gate on foot
> the job to acquaint
> those not here with deep relief
> bright fire a familiar sight

STATION 7

Hot dogs on the wharf
braised chicken cacciatore
tourists bloat North Beach
one who criticizes here
may well be ephemeral

STATION 8

Freestone fragrant baths
of cedar, rice bran, enzymes
relax the arched brow
maid wipes three times with cold cloth –
teahouse empty, priest's robe gone

STATION 9

Spiky artichokes
crown the daypicker's basket
after work he thumbs a ride
in a cape with a guitar
he rests on the strings tonight

STATION 10

> The sleeping dragon
> spills into the fluted glass
> the winemaker dreams
> at the split arbor entry
> green baubles bubbles ripen

STATION 11

> Small squares of skewered
> squid brushed with lemon herbed oil
> pinot noir signals
> by breathing to the boatman
> step ashore without spilling

STATION 12

> Sailing in the Bay
> beauty the great poets dream
> danger rescue all
> drunken tradesmen idlers popes
> lashed to poles for safe passage

STATION 13

> Keep a diary
> and a portable paint kit
> on the Tiburon ferry
> last call the City appears
> tiny puppets fans and masks

STATION 14

> Entertaining guests
> dragonflies love to alight
> on water buckets
> show off in the defense lab
> nova laser misfires

STATION 15

> Gunpowder, nothing
> electricity, nothing
> real life is random
> knife the fruit the longest day
> a going-away party

STATION 16

> Underground thunders
> when the transgendered bodies
> of clover and peach
> arrive for the ball downtown
> the only difference is time

STATION 17

> One may sigh and primp
> one may analyze one's soul
> warheads transported
> offshore glide nonstop – wake up!
> Foragers find their morels

STATION 18

> Those wishing to learn
> about the West go away
> the economy
> of the nation is kindling
> for brushfires house to house

STATION 19

Salmon rivers silt
hardwood wiped out in pain
caress the faces
gate is open peer inside
consort with an alphabet

From Time to Time
and from Place to Place

several alarms and alerts weaken the heart
the shelters fill and empty
flash! fire! heavy smoke

the desquamation of the subcutaneous tissue of half the city
poetry has no language a black outline a green wash
a red temple against snow nothing beyond

an exclamation the old story
of a young wife murdered in combat with a robber she recognizes
there is magic juggling and mime

no answer to why it is Abraham
we praise who is willing
to sacrifice his son no

way into the city
no little brown quail no leaves of the poppy

of the man who sought refuge on the steps of the Sumitomo Bank
a shadow in stone

Inspection of the Waterways

Cold sunny day
flowers arrive unexpectedly

red-tiled roofs against white clouds
from no wind to high wind in an hour

parties of young lovers by evening
metal baskets of burning kindling

the disclosure of the moon by its sentries
fireworks and cloudbursts and lanterns

crows fly past
breaking out of seclusion

a lingering passion
a world not quite of this world

flowery leaves reflected in water
one washes her brocade undergarment

Two Shops Dealing in
Tie-Dyed Fabrics

In a town famous long ago
for its field of irises and its bridge
with seven sections (like a poem!),
and an annual horse market,
and scattered clouds,

∾

I stroll on holiday with my wife.
I have brought her here for a rest,
and to buy her silk.
She works so hard
thinking, for so little,
and for untoward people
for whom even a kindness
is a mysterious thing
they dare not acquiesce to,
like a wild animal,
a monkey or deer, all day on the hunt
for chestnuts, mushrooms, and bugs.
It's true, the office has made them sad.

∾

We stroll the shops along the quay.
She takes my hand, and for that
honor I blush, and set my shoulders square,

and smile at children, for only they
aren't embarrassed by my joy.
Seven years of good luck
such that silks are sadly not enough,
but must suffice because I have spent much
on this trip already, on an inn and meals and wine.
The wine especially made my wife fiery and pure,
last night she whispered and sang
original lyrics to old tunes,
taking my name on a rhyming tour of gardens
and oceans. The sea especially made me weep,
and her, too, and in that bath we slept.

~

She begs me not approach the stall,
that already she is full.
But lemon and orange silks
and the watermelon reds of her youth
burst from a passing cloud.
So, too, her face squints in the lights,
and the owner, on one leg because of the war,
is so happy to see her
she halves the price and doubles the shawls.
I feel I know her from some other world,
but drifting (unintentionally!) to her single shoe,

I lose her glance
to a shyness.

~

My love wishes to see the irises.
Not many this year.
We muse about the weather.
At the far end,
a second shop of tie-dyed wear.
The owner, strangely, again, familiar.
This time I meet his eyes
with my heart, and recognize my father,
back from his losing war
with cancer. Father! Walter! I try
a rush of names (sailor! lover! I take him
on a rhyming tour), but he vanishes
across the first of many bridges,
which are hoisted by hand,
when a boat with high masts passes,
by men of humble birth,
scarved in baggy purple-and-green pants,
and though I run like a wave over the seven bridges
of the town, of the world,

~

he is nowhere. My wife loves me
through my loss, which because of my selfishness
she describes as a short passage from here to there
I ought to let him take alone, without thinking
that death is like dying and suffering.
This draws me ever closer to my wife.
My father's light-blue light wraps around us,
we hear distant hooves and earth quakes
as if a giant bridge is lifting. Not a single horse
but a hundred, two hundred haunches flying
and dust mingling with clouds. All eternity
in an afternoon of snorting and neighing,
nostrils of song and prayer. This is a fairy-tale
town on a route paved for an emperor,
painted in afternoon light, where the poor
wear silk because merchants give it for a song,
horses leap over water to pasture,

　　　　　　　～

and bridges rise and fall on heart and soul.
I sing my love (I take her on a rhyming tour)
among the few white irises
of poetry, most honored subject of early spring,
　　　　　　　　　　as I am,
found here romancing among lost grasses.

Note on the Cover

Japan's master print artist Andō Hiroshige immortalized scenes in all weather, seasons, and times of day along the "Eastern Sea Road," the Tōkaidō, which connected the emperor's capital in Kyoto with the seat of the shogun's administration in Edo (now Tokyo). During the golden age of preindustrial Japan, even the average citizen could undertake the adventure of travel along its popular roadway. Bad weather, or the simple desire for rest and entertainment, necessitated way stations, and the hoteliers, porters, and cooks to serve.

The thirty-five-year-old Hiroshige was sent on official business in 1832 to attend a formal event marking the presentation of horses from the shogunate to the emperor at the Kyoto Imperial Palace. He requested permission to record the gift giving, including the details of weather, wardrobe, accommodations, and meals of the procession from Edo. Hiroshige's *hanshita-e,* or print engravings, of pilgrimage ultimately take the viewer on an imaginary journey down the celebrated highway, but often had the uncanny ability to remind a traveler of his or her own trip. Although Hiroshige might heighten the weather and add nonexistent topographical features at disorienting angles, his lively enhancements rendered the perspective unorthodox with a naturalness of color and emotion that seem, even now, familiar. He also loved oversimplifying in order to distill an emotion. He might relocate sacred Mt. Fuji, which, with its perfect cone, could powerfully silence the frame, or he might reorient the highway itself to cut behind a bucolic setting. It is especially for the viewer that Hiroshige recreated the pang of regret, while packing, before leaving a stop magically darkened by rain, or the chills of excitement at the sight, through a break in the trees, of the sea.

Yui, station 17 of the Tōkaidō, depicts a page, pike bearer, umbrello, and hat bearer of one of the *daimyō,* or feudal lords, who often traveled from Edo with hundreds of servants. They are climbing toward Satta Pass, from which one could look out over Kiyomigata, a beautiful stretch of water, and see Mt. Fuji. This view omits the mountain to center a pileup of characters. Respectively, they set upon the roadway with a stride, a leg-lift, a dreaminess, and a dance. The approach wasn't nearly as steep nor as smooth, and now doesn't exist at all.

About the Author

Jane Miller's earlier collections include *Memory at These Speeds: New and Selected Poems*; *The Greater Leisures*, a National Poetry Series selection; and *August Zero*, winner of the Western States Book Award. She has also written *Working Time: Essays on Poetry, Culture, and Travel*, for the University of Michigan's Poets on Poetry Series. She is a recipient of a Lila Wallace–Reader's Digest Award for Poetry, as well as a Guggenheim Fellowship and two National Endowment for the Arts Fellowships. She lives in Tucson and is on the faculty of the Creative Writing Program at The University of Arizona.

The typeface used in this book is Minion, designed for digital composition by Robert Slimbach in 1989. Minion is classed as a neohumanist face, a contemporary typeface retaining elements of the pen-drawn letterforms developed during the Renaissance. Book cover and interior design by Valerie Brewster, Scribe Typography. Printed on Glatfelter Author's Text (acid-free, 85% recycled, 10% post-consumer stock) at McNaughton & Gunn.